Sanitarium Magazine
Issue no. 42

First Published 2016 by Sanitarium Press

This edition published 2020 by Sanitarium Publishing

ISBN 9798700683715
© 2020 Sanitarium Publishing

Facebook: https://www.facebook.com/SanitariumPublishing

Website: https://www.thesanitarium.co.uk/

2016 Edition edited by Barry Skelhorn

2020 Edition by Ian Sputnik

Thank you to all of our contributors, we couldn't have done it without you.

FACULTY MEMBERS

Dr. Sputnik
Dr. Muratori
Dr. Soldan
Dr. Algee
Dr. Marceau
Dr. Warra

Contents

ISSUE FORTY-TWO

Dear Reader,

This month we had some sad news that Richard Gladman had passed away. He was a hard working lover of all things horror. He worked tirelessly to bring old horror movies to new audiences, a magazine publisher and true patron to the arts.

He will be missed and I would like to raise a glass to this great man.

RIP Richard and thank you for taking a chance on a fledgling publication and being our first interviewee.

Barry Skelhorn

Nomi by Brooke Warra

"I told you, you can't come back here anymore, Tyler," Nomi said, dropping her keys and knapsack down on the ugly yellow kitchen counter. She shook the rain out of her hair and opened the cupboard. The window above the sink rattled against the storm raging outside.

She had known the young man would be here before she'd even unlocked her apartment door. He was always waiting for her at the kitchen table, the one with the folded up Greyhound schedule holding up one short leg. She had stopped dreaming about leaving town and decided the scrap of glossy paper could be useful if she was going to insist on keeping it. Seeing Tyler slouched at the table made her think again of pulling that brochure out and catching the next bus out of town. But then there was her son to think of. He would be out of high school in a few years. Maybe then…

"We made love on this table," Tyler said. He ran his hands lovingly over the worn hand-polished surface. "It was your mother's."

Nomi sighed and took out her old mug, the one her son had painted for her on Mother's Day ages ago, his shaky brush-strokes spelling out "World's Best Mommy". She didn't listen to Tyler reminisce as she started the water for her tea. She didn't need to; his ramblings were so predictable she knew them all by heart now.

"How is your mother, Nomi? We haven't seen her in so long…"

"She's dead, Tyler," Nomi said. She didn't turn to look at him.

"She's been dead a while now."

"Oh."

Nomi sat down across from Tyler at the table and put her head down in her arms. It had been a long night shift on the dock. The Pacific had looked fit to swallow the shore, the dancing gillnetting boats moored at the dock, and maybe the whole damn town. Nomi had finished her eight hours of security rounds with her ears ringing with the yelping of sea lions and a sticky coat of saltwater on her skin. This was winter. In the summer she would don white shorts and regale tourists on the charter boats with foolish stories about krakens.

It was a living. At just over thirty, Nomi's olive skin and thick brown hair that flopped into her eyes still gave her the look of a teenager. The married men pretending to fish and guzzling local beer liked to pinch her ass as she passed by. They left her hefty tips. She took the cash home and bought her son name brand sneakers for school. Or pizza, that rare frivolous treat. They'd eat it on the floor in front of the television and watch an old VHS tape, falling asleep on a pile of blankets there like a couple of toddlers.

Tyler was still babbling on about his undying love. Nomi snorted a laugh.

His voice quieted and in the silence the room was only full of coldness. Nomi kept her head down and pulled her damp sweater tighter around her. She knew better than to look at Tyler anymore.

"What's so funny about undying love, Nomi?" he asked. "Nothing, Tyler," she said. "But you can't come here anymore, and I'm tired, and if my son ever saw you here…"

"Your son. I want to meet him. Doesn't he ever ask about me?" Nomi pressed her forehead into the table and tried not to scream in her frustration. "Not anymore, Tyler, not for a long time," she said through gritted teeth.

"How old is he now, Nomi?"

"Sixteen. Last summer."

She thought about the spring she had been pregnant, younger in age than her son was now. She had taken the G.E.D. test and left school. She still saw her old schoolmates around town when they came to visit in the summers. They all had the same stiff hairstyles and the same personalized license plates. They were all married to the same type of man in the same polo shirt stretched over his oversized belly. They had all waited to have their children like the good church-going ladies they had been raised to be. While their sons and daughters were barely learning to ride their bicycles, Nomi's son was getting ready to apply to colleges. They heard this happy news with condescending smiles full of pity on their faces for the poor teenaged mother she had been and the poverty stricken one she was now. In her dreams, they were all closet alcoholics, hiding vodka and Ritalin in their underwear drawers.

She closed her eyes to the sudden intake of breath.

"But," Tyler said, "We'd be nearly the same age. How can I only be a few years older than your son, Nomi?"

"Exactly," she said. "That's exactly why he can't see you here." She left Tyler sitting at the table and flipped on the light in the living room. Hanging from every corner, above every window, standing on every shelf and tabletop, were dozens of handmade birdcages. Nomi had crafted them all, mostly out of old fishing twine, scraps of nets, and chicken wire. Woven in between the bars of the cages were bits of seashells, crab shells, pebbles, and driftwood she had scavenged along the beach. In a pinch she had made a few out of old clothes hangers she had scissored apart and woven together with strips of a negligee or shirt. Each one was personal, each one was unique, each one was a story. Occasionally, people on the street would come up and knock on the door and ask if they were for sale.

"No," Nomi always answered. "Never."

One persistent woman had stuck her foot in the door and offered a thousand dollars for the two in the east window. A thousand dollars! And her boy had needed braces so badly, for which she had only managed to save seventy-five dollars in the shoebox under her bed. Still, she had slammed the woman's foot in the door upon closing it. For weeks after that encounter, one particularly vocal hag had sat rattling and chittering in her cage of shells until Nomi had thought she would go mad.

A window stood open at the far end of the room causing the birdcages to rattle and swing like wind-chimes. The room was filled with a din of clacking shells and shimmering wire. One cage had fallen and lay on its side, the door of braided twigs flung open.

"A-ha," Nomi whispered. She scooped up the birdcage and checked to make sure the latch on the door still worked. It did.

She felt Tyler standing behind her. He said her name. She crooked her finger and beckoned him to follow her without turning to look at him. She would not look at him anymore.

Nomi stood outside her son's door, forcing herself to breathe slowly and swallow the bile of guilt that threatened to spew out of her. She could smell Tyler now. This was always the part she hated most, but it was the most necessary. It seemed to be the only way to get him to leave her alone. And Nomi was so tired.

She pushed the door open.

She could hear Tyler begin to cry.

"How is this possible, Nomi?" he asked. "That's not him." Nomi shook her head.

"That's him, Tyler, that's T.J., you've just been gone a long time."

In his sleep, T.J. moaned and flung an arm out as if to fend something off. Tyler was in the room.

"Tyler-No!" Nomi hissed.

He turned to her then and she could see the half of Tyler's face that had been blown away by the rudder of the boat when he'd gone overboard all that time ago. She stared into the eye bulging from the exposed meat as it rolled back and forth in crazed circles. He no longer resembled the nineteen year old boy she had once known, had once loved. Her eyes darted between the ghost and the child they shared, still asleep in his bed, unaware of the drama unfolding while he dreamt. Tyler stretched a cold, transparent hand toward T.J.'s face.

"Tyler, come away from him," she said to the broken form of her old lover. "Come away. Let me hold you."

And as he spun to greet her with open arms and an unhinged mouth, she swept the birdcage up and sent him back into its trap, roaring as he went.

She took the cage to the kitchen and stuck it behind the broom in the pantry. She would take it out on the boat tomorrow and drop it into the ocean, she thought, as she had thought a thousand times before in these last sixteen years since Tyler had first come to visit her after his death.

The sun was not yet coming up when Nomi finally rinsed the tea out of her mug, peeled off her wet clothes, and crawled into her bed. She had just started to drift off when someone began pecking insistently at her shoulder. She pulled her eye mask off, the joke kind with the funny eyes painted on them, and began choking from the stench of rot that immediately filled her lungs. She heard the birdcages in the next room rattling against each other. A few of them dropped. She had never closed the window.

Sitting by her side was an old woman in a blue nightdress, pleading with Nomi with her bloodshot, bulging eyes.

The woman gasped and tugged at the noose around her throat. "Please, can you help me get this off?"

The End.

CASE #25279

NOMI
BY BROOKE WARRA

Brooke Warra grew up and developed a deep fascination with the macabre in a fishing village in the Pacific Northwest with her very Finnish family. She writes and lives with her two children near Phoenix, Arizona. She has been previously published in Under The Bed Magazine and has a writing prompt ebook available on Amazon.

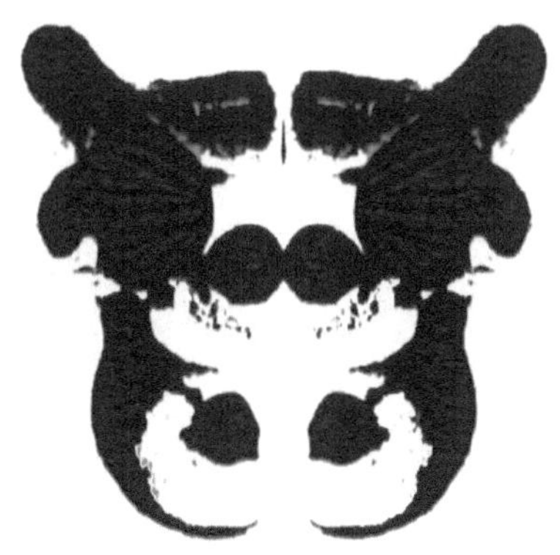

Caretakers by Andrew Jurisic

On the day of Kinnon's arrival, a bridge collapsed out in Shreveport.

Far enough away that there was no particular dread we knew any of the 27 who died, but close enough to mute jubilation into circumspect celebration.

He was an infant, like any other. Adorable, a little tuft of soft, black hair. Smelled like strawberries and maple syrup and a cold fireplace.

His eyes wide, staring. Intelligent and searching.

An infant, like any other.

I suppose I had had the occasional thought about the bridge collapse since, but I had forgotten the connection to Kinnon's birth date.

***

He grew with purpose. Like he had somewhere important to be and couldn't bother with formalities.

At the age of 5, Kinnon had the strength of a 12-year-old. His mother and I noticed, but few others did; he kept to himself, for the most part. He had no interest in pushing other kids around, nor indeed in joining their play.

Silent and watchful. That was Kinnon. Always watching with those large, intelligent eyes.

His vocabulary developed well. People who met him at the grocery store or at the house would say things like, "Well you're quite the old soul, aren't you?"

Kinnon never smiled, and seemed not to take pleasure in things we expect kids to take pleasure in. He tried ice cream one time, and declined it thereafter. He didn't care for kid food - no chicken fingers or fish sticks for Kinnon - nor did he care for food in general.

He ate what we ate, and found no joy in it.

He read books. Picture books, at first. Helpful rabbits and kind bears. They failed to maintain his attention for long, and he never re-read anything, as I had seen other kids do.

He read young adult fiction for a time, and soon started on the encyclopedia. And to say he enjoyed anything at all would be pure projection, but he was harder to distract at times. After a while, I noticed he seemed more engrossed when reading about particular subjects.

***

A few of our friends had had children before Penelope and I. We used to laugh about how parents would identify regular, ordinary things in their children and interpret them as hallmarks of uniqueness -- greatness, even. "Oh, Eustace just loves to lick crayons. He has an extraordinary palate. He'll be a talented chef one day."

New parents also wish to convince themselves of their own greatness. Their own specialness. They want to believe not that they have a regular, normal kid, but that there's something exceptional about their child. And hence, something exceptional about them as parents. "I may have achieved nothing above the mediocre my entire life, but in producing offspring, I finally prove my greatness." I'm sure you know the types. On one end of that scale, there are parents who put excessive pressure on their children to be marvelous. On the other end of the scale, there are parents who take delight in children who manifest rare diseases, disorders, or allergies. It's a ghoulish truth, but some parents delight in complex, sick children for the attention it earns them.

Penelope and I observed our friends' various parenting delusions and determined to avoid their mistakes. We wanted to be different. We had no desire for an exceptional child; normal and healthy was just fine by us. We had no desire to imprint their lives with our dreams, and resolved to be supportive, encouraging parents who took a serious approach to discipline.

We talked about Kinnon, who had zero use for encouragement, or support, or even discipline. We agreed Kinnon was not the kind of child we had expected, but was he abnormal? Unlikely. The greater likelihood, we agreed, was that some desire in us for an un-ordinary child had somehow still manifested itself. Like our friends, we were looking hard for something exceptional in Kinnon. It was inadvertent, but we were putting pressure on him to be odd, to satisfy our need for him to be interesting. That was it. It must be.

I worried Kinnon perceived some of this pressure. Had internalized it, somehow. We had been sending confusing signals to our child. And we had failed to understand their effects on him.

'Kinnon, how do you feel?' I said, surprised I had never asked my sensitive, intelligent, articulate son before.

Kinnon never looked up. He continued reading, absorbed in the encyclopedia.

'Kinnon? Kinnon.'

He looked up. I caught the heading on the entry in the open book: "Genocide".

'Kinnon, how do you feel?'

He stared for a minute. Still, watchful. And then he said, 'I feel fine, daddy' and went back to his reading.

He felt fine. Still, I resolved to ask him once a day, from then on.

I wanted to be there for him, to make sure he was alright.

And some days I forgot, or was too busy, so there was no great consistency to my inquiries. But every time I asked, Kinnon would respond the exact same way: I feel fine, daddy.Same words, same monotone, same pause. Like a rehearsed line, delivered to perfection. But he felt fine. He felt fine, daddy.

***

I found myself reading books about parenting. Parenting sensitive children. I couldn't talk about my concerns with other parents, or with professionals. The last thing I wanted, unlike those attention-seeking parents, was for others to think Kinnon abnormal.

I read one after the other. None of them gave me a complete picture, but each one gave me a piece of it. It was painstaking, but I was assembling a complete picture of-

'David!'

'What?! What do you want?'

Penelope recoiled, wounded. 'How can you snap at me like that? I was loud, but I called you four times!'

'Pen, I'm sorry, I was just concentrating….'

'Fuck you, David. And fuck your apology.'

I closed the book, stood, put my hands on her shoulders. 'Pen, I'm sorry. Pen. Look at me. I'm sorry. I'm so sorry. I'm an asshole.'

'Fine', she said.

'Pen, are you ok?'

She turned, shrugging my hands off her shoulders. 'I'm fine,' she said.

I had snapped, and I felt terrible about it. I had apologized, but it was going to take some serious work to climb out of this doghouse.

Penelope is a warm, honest person, and she finds it difficult to hide her feelings. She was still hurt, still upset, still cold to me. And nothing gave me discomfort like hearing those two chilling words from her: 'I'm fine'. Meaning, anything but.

I'm fine.

I feel fine, daddy.

***

I rolled Penelope's suitcase out to the car and watched her back out of the driveway. It had taken some fierce apologies, and genuine remorse, but she had forgiven my snapping at her. We were good, again.

She was off to the coast for the weekend, and I envied her not a whit: surrounded by real estate agents for three days, sitting through presentations and self-congratulatory speeches and nonsense awards.

I had a lot of work to do this weekend, myself. But first things first.

'Kinnon,' I said. 'How do you feel?'

Pause. Glance up. Encyclopedia open: Hitler. 'I feel fine, daddy.' 'No, Kinnon. "Fine" isn't going to cut it. I want to know how you feel, okay? I want you to describe how you're feeling, in a way that I can understand. Okay?' I remembered something from the book I'd last read. 'If it helps, why don't you draw me a picture about how you feel?' I looked at his neat-stacked building blocks. 'Or build something? You take some time and think about it, and we'll talk again in an hour, ok?'

'OK, daddy.'

***

I had written the first paragraph of my report when the digital clock on my desk beeped the hour. I looked up and remembered my commitment. I rose from the desk and turned to find him standing in the doorway, watching me.

'Kinnon. Are you ready, buddy?'

'Yes, daddy.' He turned and left, and I followed.

He went to the back door, turned the knob, and slipped out onto the patio. I followed. He stepped off the patio and walked through the backyard. I followed.

When he reached the far end of the backyard, he walked around behind a live oak and I walked around, too.

Kinnon pointed at the base of the tree. 'Here's how I feel, daddy.' At the base of the tree, a pile of sticks. The remains of a nest a pair of doves had built in the spring. The sticks were broken and splintered. Four or five doves' eggs were smashed against the base of the tree, pieces of shell and slimy yolk clinging to the bark.

To the left and right of the broken twigs lay two adult doves, male and female, their necks twisted at strange angles. They looked ragged, as though someone with small, brutal feet had stomped on them over and over and over and over.

***

Two nights I lay awake. I wondered how it had come to this, how I had managed to isolate myself from every source of support. I had no one to call for advice, commiseration, or just to listen to me. I had expected my life would be different at this point. Better.

I stopped asking Kinnon how he felt. I didn't know what any of it meant, but something was very wrong with my son. Had I done that? Had I driven him to such a point of distress that he had to act out?

We would have to spend more time with Kinnon. Build his self-confidence, give him whatever he needed. Perhaps a baby sister, to give him some perspective. I would discuss it with Penelope when she returned in ... an hour! She was on her way back. I had almost forgotten.

'Kinnon', I said. 'Are you hungry?'

Pause. Glance up. Encyclopedia open: Holocaust. 'I feel fine, daddy.'

I bent and picked up the volume. Kinnon's eyes narrowed. 'That's enough of that for now, Kinnon. How about some rabbits and bears, huh?'

'I don't want the rabbits and bears, daddy.'

'How about some cartoons? How about acting more like a normal fucking kid?' I regretted it as soon as I said it. I could feel hot tears welling at the corners of my eyes.

'I don't want to be a normal fucking kid, daddy. Give me back my fucking book.'

'No,' I said. 'No more disasters. No more wars. No more horrors. No more feeding whatever it is inside you that you're feeding. We have to starve it, don't you see?'

I ran to the front door, Kinnon coming after me. 'Give me back my fucking book!' he hissed.

'No!'

I threw open the front door, ran out into the yard. Kinnon jumped and tried to grab the book, but I held it out of his reach. He kicked me, clawed, scratched and spat.

I tossed the book as far as I could. It went spinning out, over the road, and into the small woods on the other side.

Kinnon took off after it, though he had never tried to cross the road before. He stepped onto the asphalt. I heard the screech of tires before I ever noticed the car. Penelope's Taurus.

The ambulance arrived with all haste, but Kinnon was long gone. The massive shock to his tiny body had caused his instantaneous death.

Penelope was numb, shocked. But she also felt a relief I could see in her eyes, recognize in myself, and of which we would never speak.

***

'David, I'm pleased to see you back this week. I still think there's something valuable you can gain from this process', said Dr. Frantz.

'Thanks, Doctor.'

'How are you feeling today? Any different? Any more feelings of guilt, or relief?'

Well, Dr. Frantz. How to tell you how I feel today?

You know the paramedics tended to Penelope as a precaution, after the accident. They took her to hospital with a mild concussion.

You also know that a doctor at the hospital discovered her pregnancy.

You know Penelope is now 4 months pregnant and she is decided on the name Kenzie for our daughter.

You know we buried Kinnon in a peaceful place, on a green hill. What you don't know is that the flowers we put on Kinnon's grave wither and die overnight.

You don't know that on Penelope's first ultrasound everything looked normal to the doctor and Penelope. And they looked away to talk about blood test results, and for just a second as I looked at the screen, I swear I saw a tail.

What you don't know is, in her first trimester, I would wake at night to hear whispers coming from her belly.

You don't know that for the last month, I have dreamed every night. Vivid dreams of blood and fire and a rider on an emaciated horse.

You don't know that three nights ago, I woke in the garage. Two nights ago, I woke in the garage, pouring gasoline into a can.

And last night I woke over Penelope as she slept, gasoline can in my left hand, lit match in my right.

You don't know that I want to punch your office wall with both fists, over and over and over and over until my hands are mangled, bloody messes of flesh and broken, protruding bones and I want to hold them under your nose and say, 'This. This is how I feel!'

'David?'

I looked out the windows, at a bare tree bending in a gentle, cold wind.

'I feel fine, Dr. Frantz.'

A pair of doves alit in the upper branches.

I feel fine.

The End.

CASE #16462

CARETAKERS

BY ANDREW JURISIC

Andrew Jurisic is a writer from Melbourne, Australia, living and working in New York.

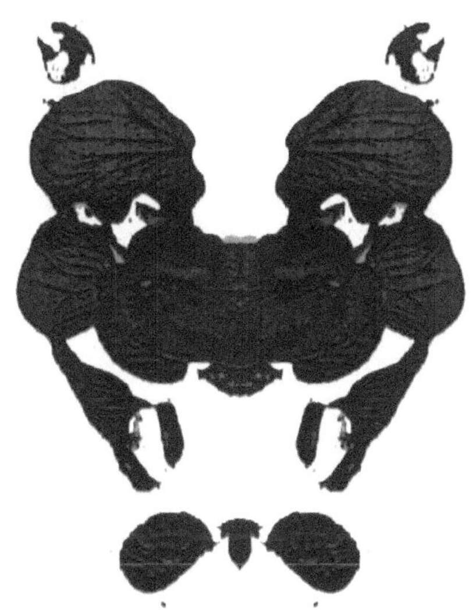

Picture This by Ian Mullins

Daylight died. There was the usual town square, flags fluttering like children waving from trains, but the webcam was dark and thick-grained. Colin glanced down at the date and time, and saw that the camera had frozen at two-thirty in the morning, four hours earlier.

Disappointed, he travelled to Stockholm instead. Sometimes he could watch the river for hours, small boats jerking across the screen in thirty second intervals, leaping like ballerinas across a puddle of sweat deposited on the stage. But a notice lit up his laptop, informing him that the camera would be down for three months while the restaurant that housed it was re-designed. He snapped back to Scotland, but the night was still a painting daubed by fingerprints, flags frozen in mid-flutter. One man still strode across the street leading down to the harbour, a dark cartoon clad in a long coat that almost reached his ankles.

But something felt wrong; a detail had changed without his knowledge. He scrutinized the clock by the flag, the haze of damp red light from the cash machine outside the bank. But the night was as brilliantly alone as he was.

Dispirited, he flew to New York, but could see nothing but snow. He turned back to Scotland. Same flags, same gale. But the man in the greatcoat had gone.

He checked the date and time; the webcam was still frozen solid. He was viewing ancient history, but the man had vanished into the footlights. Or was that him, lounging in a shadow outside the blackened bakery? There was a tiny pin of light near his face, as though he was lighting a cigarette; but the face was just a blur, a photograph from a newspaper left out in the rain.

Startled, but curiously excited, Colin journeyed to Canada, then Australia. He allowed ten minutes to slowly dissolve like a pill on his tongue, then rushed back to Scotland. The hour was still locked, but the man had vanished completely. Or was he the slight smudge on the left of the screen, as though he stood just below the camera, and was in the act of covering it up?

This time Colin stayed away for half an hour, visiting Venice and Malmo, foot tapping away the seconds. When he returned Scotland had gone, blanketed in what appeared to be a thick grey fog. It took several minutes to convince himself that the man had thrown his coat over the camera. What did he have to hide?

What does anyone have to hide? Colin had nothing, a fact that he went to great lengths to hide.

He checked his watch. Daylight clocked him on. He threw on clothes and cold water, strapped shoes like paddles to his feet, then waded out into the world. Work washed over him like a slow tide over a man chained to a harbour wall. He pressed keys, spoke into a telephone. Or rather his fingers pressed keys, his voice spoke into a telephone. He himself was unmoved, un-chained. His mind was in Belfast and Oban.

Home-time came slowly, his train even more so. Other people boarded with him, but he barely noticed they were alive, a compliment they were happy to re-pay. As soon as he was home he threw off his coat as though discarding a dead body he'd carried on his back all day, flourishing the laptop into life like plastic roses hidden up his sleeve.

Scotland came alive. For a moment he was curiously disappointed to find that the webcam had been re-booted, that falling sun now fell on the square. His eyes instinctively searched the edges of the image for a shadow man in a shadow coat, but he was nowhere. But then he saw that the centre of the image, below the quiet flags, had changed. A bright red tent had been raised on the traffic island, surrounded by soft yellow tape. Smudged men in smudged uniforms attended to its needs.

Colin watched for the next three hours while suits came and went, flags rose and fell. A small crowd gathered, silently murmuring, across the street. Together they watched the crinkled body-bag smothered away.

Her name was Rachel, he discovered later. He couldn't remember her second name. She was an architect, or someone who worked for one. Her throat had been cut and her wrists opened, as though in a parody of suicide. Entranced, Colin read every detail, immediately forgetting all of them.

Over dinner spooned from a paper plate beside his laptop, he pondered the actions he knew he should take. He should contact the police, or the press. Tell his 'story'. That was already how it felt to him. It was his story, not Rachel's, or the shadow-man's. He finally had a tale to tell, and he carefully planned how he might tell it, building long and complex scenarios in his shadowed mind. Most of them ended with him quietly walking away in a trench coat while the shadow man screamed after him, the police cuffing him into a waiting van. He felt a mother's tears on his cheek, the firm handshake of a father. Perhaps a younger brother's nod of respect.

The week limped by. At work he was even less aware than usual, sometimes putting down telephones in the middle of conversations, addressing letters for London with a Scottish postcode. He called his boss Rachel. She reminded him to take his medication. At home he barely slept, except at his computer. He watched strangers leaving tributes of flowers, and a florist stealing them for her front window. Men photographed badly-rhymed poems wrapped in plastic bags. Women brushed away theatrical tears.

On Saturday morning Colin was surprised to find himself in a train travelling to Scotland. He barely recalled going to the station or buying a ticket. He was living a story at last. The green hills and lochs were no less real to him than the loops of story that reeled endlessly through his head. Rachel would turn to him and kiss him, blood gaping from her wrists and throat. At Glasgow, where he believed he had to change trains, he decided to go without food until the story ended. His body was a distant maze of churning sensations and impolite requests. His mind was just the same.

Soon he smelled the sea he'd only ever imagined before. With no bags and no coat, his only luggage his laptop, he climbed down from the train and tried to discover how far it was to the square. Uncertain, he opened up Google Earth and discovered it was only yards away. A corner shop had a new sign, a green door was now painted red. He followed in imaginary footsteps. New streets led into familiar shapes and corners, now livid and large, broken brick and loose stone. It was beyond him, and he was glad.

Soon he stood in Argyll Square itself. Flags fluttered continuously; the cash machine had many visitors. The flowers on the traffic island were worn and grey; the poems withered, the visitors few.

It took him a few minutes to find his place, the tiny webcam tucked into the corner of a shop selling tartan-patterned guitars and saxophone-shaped bottle-openers. He edged forward and back, left and right, searching for the correct position. He tried not to think that people looking at the webcam might see him there, laptop clutched to the chest like an armoured breast-plate. He closed his eyes for thirty seconds at a time, then snapped them open, just to be sure. When people tried to speak to him he closed his eyes and failed to speak. He didn't work for them; he owed them nothing. He offered silence, his finest gift. They walked away, muttering.

Soon it grew dark. A thick, blotchy fingerprint pressed on the edges of his vision. Light leaked through the eyelids; car-engines brayed in his ears. In his mind he pressed 'mute'. After thirty seconds he opened his eyes, knowing exactly what he would see. A shadow in a greatcoat crossed the harbour road, face like a smudged newspaper photograph left out in the rain. Colin smiled to himself, sealing his eyes again. The life he'd dreamt of was finally unfolding. At last, nothing made sense.

The next time he looked out he saw nothing but grey, as though a coat had been thrown over his face. He was vaguely aware of a hand in his -perhaps it was Rachel's- tenderly leading him away from the street down narrow alleys that grew narrower every time he opened his eyes and peered through buttonholes; alleys so narrow that it seemed that nothing human could pass through them. He wondered who had built such passageways. Perhaps those who believed in absence, like himself.

He awoke to a small dull room, much like his own, with a single laptop, identical to his. Between intervals of necessary darkness, he stared at the frozen image on the screen. It showed the familiar square, the frozen flags, the broken red light, but a shadow kept moving. Every time he opened his eyes the shadow stretched again. A dull figure in a greatcoat, much like the one he'd always wanted, but had never owned. The face was flat and dull, much like the one he himself wore.

In time another shadow joined it, their bodies edging together until they merged into one indistinguishable shadow. The next time he looked both had gone, and it had begun to rain. The webcam was an old clock running backwards.

The greatcoat entered the room with silver flashes at his throat and hands. Colin was unsurprised to see that even from a distant of six feet, now three feet, now inches, his face was that of a newspaper photograph left out in the rain.

The End.

CASE #53733

PICTURE THIS

34

BY IAN MULLINS

Ian Mullins throws in the towel from Liverpool, England. He has published stories with Brand, Massacre, Hellfire Crossroads and The Literary Hatchet. His poetry collection Laughter In The Shape Of A Guitar is available from UB (undergroundbooks.org).

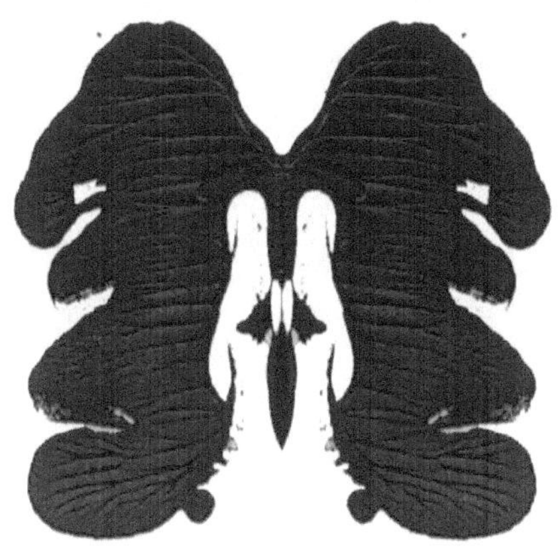

Soft Cell by Sean Spagnoli

Every sink in the apartment is obstructed by either dishes or hair. Panties hang in a row from the shower rod like parti-colored bats. Bills rise in drifts from the kitchen table. Emma pokes at one and the sound of plastic address windows sliding past each other is like the whisper of snakes through dead leaves.

Emma sighs as the envelopes fall *plap plap plap* to the floor.

She is a terrible roommate.

Is she also a terrible girlfriend? That's the really big question. That's the kicker.

Until she'd moved in with Susan, that hadn't really been an issue. They'd been great together—charming at parties, happy when alone…fucking fantastic in bed. It wasn't until three months ago when they'd begun cohabitating that things had started going downhill.

Some folks were not meant to share a living space with literally any other human being. The idea that loving a person meant you had to permanently inhabit a couple of rooms with them was just… *rude*, honestly. Primitive.

Ideally, in a millennium, we'd all live alone in super sci-fi bubbles that could temporarily fuse with our girlfriends' bubbles. That way, we could hang out and watch movies and fuck and then separate like civilized human beings. In a thousand years, being slow on the uptake for dish duty or bathroom cleaning would be no big fucking deal. In a thousand years, we'd have flying cars and not even the red states would give two shits about inter-lady kissing. In a thousand years, Emma might learn how to fold her own laundry.

But for now, she chews a fingernail and glares at the couch. "Okay, I realize I'm an absolute trash person, but does ANYONE need this many fucking pillows?" she asks herself. "What does it say about a woman that she needs this many pillows?" Emma stands at the far corner of the room, staring at the couch pregnant with throw pillows of various shapes, sizes, and colors. "Does Sue have a back problem? She'd have told me by now, I guess. It'd be stupid for her not to. I don't even remember her buying half of these...I wonder if she's been mall-cheating on me."

Emma sighs, and spits the fingernail onto the carpet.

"I smoke too much. Scramblin' my eggs is all," she says, tapping her forehead. She stands for a moment, nodding to herself, eyes flicking over the room. "I'm gonna do it," she sighs, "I'm gonna clean this motherfucker up before Sue gets back from DC. I am an unstoppable machine...I am Rosy the goddamn Robot...I am..."

Dishes in the sink, papers on the table, tumbleweeds of hair and dust in the corners.

"I am definitely not doing this sober."

Moments later, she's sitting on the edge of the couch packing a bowl with a glass of Chianti on deck. She never really used to drink wine before Sue—she'd been more of a liquor-that-comes-in-a plastic-bottle kind of gal—but she'd gotten all classed up, just like everything else Sue touched. The wine, watching her potty mouth, the "better" job...just like the throw pillows, Sue loved adding all these little touchups, as if nothing was ever good enough on its own.

But then again, it wasn't as if she couldn't use *some* improvement. Everybody can be just a little bit better, right? Wait...that's Sue's line, isn't it?

"Ugggh, get out of my head!" Emma groans, flicking the little orange plastic lighter and taking a deep pull. She holds it in her lungs, watching smoke curl towards the ceiling. Sue doesn't really mind her smoking in the apartment as long as...

"Shit!" she coughs, gouts of smoke subsuming the finer tendrils from the bowl. She stands up suddenly and opens the window behind the couch. She then rushes to the other side of the room and turns on the little air filter fan thingy Sue insists on making her use.

Crisis averted. Domestic fucking bliss.

She goes to flop back on the couch and is surprised at how upright she remains.

"Fucking pillows," she mutters, turning on the television. She flips around for a bit before landing on a pair of breasts. Interest piqued, she lights up again and holds it in her lungs. She's seen it before. It's not porn…well, not exactly. It's some British flick from the 80s with space vampires. And breasts. A winning combination.

Sue's not into porn, or science fiction or horror for that matter. Emma hates the term "chick flick," she finds it demeaning, but seriously, there are only so many romantic comedies you can watch before you want to strangle every last pretty straight couple on the planet. Sue loves that stuff—loves rich white people with insultingly simple problems, loves Cinderella stories where Cinderella can afford a three-bedroom apartment in Brooklyn with only one roommate, loves happy endings. Uncomplicated, cliché, "I gotta catch the train before he leaves forever because it's not like the internet exists," happy endings.

She blows a smoke ring at the derelict spaceship on TV. It looks like a big, wrinkly spacedick. She snorts and laughs to herself, lying back (as far as she can, at least) on the pillows. Gazing up at the ceiling, she thinks about Sue. Beautiful, blonde, girly-girl Sue. Corn-fed, white-bred, and drop-dead gorgeous. Smart, too. Genius-level smart, Emma suspects. She'd graduated from some flyover state college (Flyover State—God, if only it was actually called that) with a Bachelor's in...something corporately feasible...Emma can't remember what, exactly. She'd then been almost immediately snapped up by some skyrocketing interior design company with an office right on the water. Hence the nice apartment. Hence her absence for some big conference in DC.

Hence the pillows.

There'd been no argument about who would move in with whom—Emma had shared a furnished closet with two other girls and a phalanx of roaches for most of their relationship. Almost a year now. Shit, she has to get something for the anniversary. Shit, it should probably be expensive.

Shit.

Moving in after seven months together. That had been...weird. Hell, the whole relationship had been weird. Stunning as she was, Susan hadn't really been Emma's type. Before Susan, Emma had been into boyish girls, girlish boys, trans and nonbinary folks... anyone queer...anyone who didn't fit neatly into a slot.

Fitting into slots. She giggled and sipped her wine.

Then along came Susan.

They'd met at a bar in the way that people meet at bars. Emma had noticed her perfume first and bought her a drink, even though she couldn't afford it. They'd got to talking and she was just so strong and feminine and...and what? So *attractive*, that was it. It sounds glib, but physicality aside, there's always been something magnetic about Susan. Always the center of a crowd...impossible to ignore in private. Ten months later, and boom: Emma's slowly sinking into an ocean of lumpy- ass pillows while getting tore up on wine, weed, and naked space vampires.

And it had all started with that perfume. Despite having been together for ten months, Sue had never let on what it was called, and damned if she wasn't hiding it like a superspy. Nothing in the medicine cabinet...no possible combination of those things smelled like Susan, yet Susan smelled like it all the time. Emma had asked (easy birthday present, perfume), but the conversation always ended up miles away from a straight answer. Whatever... Emma probably can't afford it anyway.

The naked lady space vampire is making out with some hapless soldier boy and turning him into a mummy. "Good for you, girl.

Suck that bitch dry," Emma says, raising her glass to the television.

God, Susan would *hate* this flick. Susan hates most of the things Emma is into, and, if she's being honest, vice versa. They have so little in common, Emma can't fathom how they get along so well... or *got* along so well before moving in together. She sighs, casting a forlorn glance at the sink. There's a casserole dish half sunk, titanic-like, into the pile that's been there since just before Susan had left a few days ago. The cheese and potatoes lining the bottom are probably cement by now, and she'll have to soak it first. To soak it, she'll have to clear the sink by doing the rest of the dishes.

Existence is futile and we all die alone, she thinks to herself, finishing the wine in a single gulp. Still, she really should at least do the dishes—she thinks back to her old apartment and the roaches. An infestation is the last thing this apartment or their relationship needs.

That, and kids. Funny she should think of kids and cockroaches at the same time. Sue definitely wants kids...Emma is reasonably sure that is not the case for the cockroaches. Once they'd moved in together, babies and marriage seemed to be all Susan could talk about. It was like Emma had tripped a switch crossing the threshold. All of a sudden it was weddings and kids and family planning followed by retirement, senescence, and, promptly, death.

No thank you, Ma'am.

Biologically, once you passed on your genes, you raised your kids until they were old enough to do the same, and then you died. Your purpose as a placental mammal was complete and you were no longer of use even to your own DNA. In Emma's mind, the key to immortality was to never, ever, breed.

That's what a lot of their most recent fights had been about. Susan said she came from a big, traditional family, which, to Emma, was no kind of argument at all. Susan's clan had already contributed enough to the gene pool, so she should really just give it a rest already.

Needless to say, Sue's parting for DC had been more sorrowful than sweet.

Emma feels a pang of guilt as the mummy-man resurrects on screen. Despite his brown, withered flesh, his eyes are shockingly blue, like Susan's.

The least Emma can do is clean up while she's gone…make some kind of peace. Even though she's definitely not up for becoming… gravid…she might consider adoption. Might. Consider it. That's all she can promise.

"But before we begin…" she says, reaching for the lighter.

It isn't there.

It isn't on the table next to the empty wine glass and it isn't in the pocket of her jeans or her robe. It isn't on the floor and she hasn't kicked it under the couch. She could swear…

It's in the pillows.

She's sure of it. It must have fallen out of her pockets. She looks at the mountain of them, realizing suddenly that she's spent this whole time sitting on the only six to ten inches of couch seat that's not subsumed by the multicolored avalanche.

"Fffffuck."

Her eyes roam over them for a solid minute, trying to decide on the best plan of attack. Sure, she could throw them all on the floor, but the floor is gross. Like really, really gross. Like bus station bathroom gross. She can't throw them on the floor until she vacuums, and that's not in the cards for at least the next 48 hours. She takes a deep breath. If she can just slide her hands under the mound and feel around for it, it can't be that far in. It's not like she moved around that much, right?

She kneels on the gross floor, feeling grit and hair under the skin of her legs. She grimaces and regards the wall of pillows before her. Most of these must be free samples from Sue's design conferences…they have to be. Each is unique and not one of them matches another, the couch, or anything else in the apartment. There are familiar ones at the front of the line, not like old friends, exactly, but more like the people who run the bank or the grocery store: Square Denim, Round Muslin, Pink Fur Cylinder. These she moves aside, rapidly filling up whatever couch space exists to either side of her sitting dent.

The second layer is a bit stranger. She remembers seeing these before, but they'd been covered up by the more comfortable old worthies, with good reason. One is covered with oversized buttons made from coconut shell. Another is lined with inch-wide, pink sequins that looked like the scales of some Antediluvian homosexual. The Elder Liberace sits next to a lump encrusted with purple plastic gem stones.

"Gross," she mutters, sliding her hand in under the purple thing. Without being able to see, the couch cushion underneath

(Emma's couch, the only piece of her *own* furniture that Sue had let her move in to the apartment) is her reference point. The textures of the pillows that she can't see brush against the top of her hand, and as she goes deeper, they get more and more confusing. She can recognize buttons (why would you ever put a button on a pillow? What would you possibly button to it?) and rhinestones and ruffles, but there are other things. Things that feel cool and hard like seashells or smooth and ridged like alligator skin or thin and dry and whispery like…

"FUCK!" she shrieks, yanking her hand out and clutching it to her chest. Blood spills from the top of her hand in warm, red rivulets, welling out and over onto Pink Fur Cylinder, staining its plush hide. She runs over to the kitchen sink and, seeing it's still full, she runs to the bathroom. Cold water. Soap. It stings like a motherfucker. Like that time she'd been on the slide in kindergarten and the hollow aluminium frame had contained a hornet's nest. "What the fuck," she hisses, looking down at what she expects to be a huge gash. Some fatal wound that will kill her slowly before the paramedics get there. At least she'll make a beautiful corpse.

But there isn't one. It hurts like there should be, but after the blood is washed away, there's nothing. Well, almost nothing. Just past the closest knuckle of her middle finger, sitting right on top of a vein (God, she's getting old lady hands, isn't she?) sits a tiny, red welt, no bigger than a pinprick. Still and all though, whenever she moves it out of the stream of water, the blood comes again, fast and sure.

Holding it under the faucet, dazed by what has just happened, she opens the medicine cabinet and rifles around before finding a box of Band-Aids and a tube of antibiotic ointment. Pulling the little paper tabs off with her teeth, she squeezes some goo onto the pad and covers the wound. She rests with her head down, leaning heavily over the sink and listening to the running water.

In a minute, she sniffs and rises, shutting off the water. She runs to her bedroom and picks up the biggest dictionary she can find and stalks back towards the couch. It can't have been broken glass or anything like that…there would have been a bigger cut. Christ, was it a needle or something? No…that was ridiculous; this was Susan's apartment, not the Jersey shore. That left…fuck, that left either rats or bugs.

Rats or bugs. Fuck.

She holds the dictionary in her uninjured hand since the other one tingles and throbs. There's the couch with the pillows. There's the remote, the baggie, the wine glass. No signs of creepy crawlies.

Yet.

She lifts up pillows one by one as if performing an excavation, holding the dictionary in her rapidly-tiring left hand. Down and down and down layers of colors and patterns and textures and shapes. It's like watching one of those weird oil-pattern projections from the seventies they used to use in movie theaters. It makes her slightly nauseous.

She's hit bottom. She can see the couch…see the lighter…see the culprit.

A small, rectangular, black leather pillow, studded with metal spikes. She stares at it. A punk rock pillow. A Punk. Fucking. Rock. Pillow.

What the fuck.

What fevered brain, what twisted hell-spawned mind though anyone…*anyone* would need a pillow with fucking *spikes* on it?

She retrieves the lighter, sliding it into her pocket before reaching down and gingerly gripping one of the conical metal studs. She dangles it in front of her like some dead thing caught in a trap. None of the spikes look sharp enough to break skin, but there's nothing else there: No rats, no bugs, no nest of scorpions. (*Do they even have scorpions here? Hell if I know.*)

"Fuck this pillow!" she screams, tossing it out the open window.

She half-wishes it'll hit someone on the way down.

Emma is on her second bowl of the evening…her fourth glass of wine. On the television, London is fucked. Proper fucked, they'd say over there. Vampire zombies are everywhere and they are shooting lasers out of their faces…or something.

"Proper fucked," She mumbles. That's what she is, all right… proper fucked.

Her right hand hurts less, now, but the throbbing persists and when she holds it up to the flickering screen it looks bigger than the left. Then again, she's high as shit, so who is she to judge?

She's piled Sue's pillows up to either side of her and she sits on her own couch, on her own cushions like Moses parting the red sea.

So many pillows.   Too many fucking pillows.   Why would anyone need so many pillows?

The thought comes to her unbidden and she freezes. *Pillows are generally used to smother people.*

She shudders and takes another deep drag. Speaking of pillows…fuck. Pink Fur Cylinder must look like a Pink Fur Massacre after she bled all over it. She leans forward and gropes for it, lacing her fingers through its fur. It feels oddly warm as she rolls it over in her hands, blinking fishily. In the glow of the television, there's no blood. Maybe she just *thought* she'd bled on it? Right now, though, it seems fine. Cleaner than before. Bigger, maybe. She chuckles and hugs it like a stuffed animal.

"Proper fucked," she squeals.

Emma tosses the pillow aside and lies back. The television is screaming. What is she doing here? What is she doing in Susan's apartment—sorry, *their* apartment? Why the hell did she move in with that bitch? No, that's terrible. Susan isn't a bitch…

But…

But she kind of is.

Why, when she talks about Emma's acting career it always comes out sounding like "career" ?

Why does every decision about furniture or friends or dinner begin and end with Susan?

Why is she here?

And then she remembers.

Before Susan, she was hand-to-mouth. She could barely make rent and health insurance was about as likely as a personal mission to Mars.

Before Susan, she hadn't been able to hold down a job for more than three months. Now, she's doing the whole secretary thing (care of the Great and Powerful Susan) and is making, like, thousands of dollars more than she's ever made before. Doesn't leave much time for auditions, though…not that Susan cares.

Before Susan, she was happy.

No, that's not right.

That's not…

Is it, though?

When's the last time she's gone out and had a good time, like, a *really* good time?

She can't even remember. Can she? She thinks back…wayyy way back, to an old roommate. She's distracted. Her body feels heavy…heavy like lead…but her head feels light. Her brain is floating up and out and away. She feels sweaty and sick to her stomach. She is lying back. On the television there are laser beams flying into space. Ghosts. Screaming. Too much screaming. She looks around her.

The pillows are breathing.

Are they breathing? Noooo no fucking way. They're not breathing. They're not...

They're not moving on their own. It's just because she's sitting back so heavy and she piled them up to high—they're getting close because she's sinking back. She overdid it. Weed and wine and nothing in her stomach to soak it up, God, what if she pukes on the pillows? What if she pukes lying back and she-*Suffocates.*

She stirs and blinks as the pillows, the warm pillows start falling....as the walls start crumbling into her lap. They smell like Susan. All of them smell like Susan. It actually feels pretty nice. She feels good. She feels safe. That's not something she's had a lot of in her life—safety. There's one more thought as they pile up up up and over her. As they really *do* start to breathe. As they start to chirp softly, like crickets wrapped in cotton.

She has one last thought. What had her friend said...what was it she'd said about safety?

Safety is a trap.

London screams and things go dark.

Susan unlocks the door and steps into the apartment. It's always strange, smelling your rooms after you've been away for a while. The human sense of smell has an exquisite ability to adapt to "normal" odors in order to sense danger. It's easy to forget what home smells like.

Right now, home smells like the dishes haven't been done in two weeks...like the carpet hasn't been vacuumed, and the window's been left open.

Susan shakes her head, setting her rolling bag by the door and pulling it shut. The locks click into place and she surveys her domain. Unsurprisingly, Emma has done nothing to clean up. In fact, Susan is pretty sure the sink and the carpet are in worse shape than before she left. She shakes her head and leans against the door. It's been a long journey. She rubs her hands over her shoulders, her breasts, her belly.

Behind the couch, the curtains sway in the breeze from the open window. On the table, there is a bottle of wine, an empty glass, and an open bag of weed. Susan rolls her eyes and begins tidying up, finding the lighter and the pipe on the floor. She pulls the dust buster from its wall charger and quickly sucks the ash off the floor and the stray crumbs from the table. The wine bottle is empty.

The television is still on…giant, man-faced ants in black and white. She shuts it off.

In all her dither to clean the living room, she hasn't really taken the time to look at Emma's hideous couch. There, taking up the remaining six to ten inches of free cushion, is a body pillow that she's never seen before—it's white and fluffy and inviting. A beatific grin splits her face.

Susan is so tired from the journey, so tired from everything that's happened over the past two weeks. She could use a good sleep in her own bed. Gingerly, she leans over and hefts the body pillow onto her shoulder.

It is heavier than it looks.

Then again, Susan is stronger than she looks.

Once in the bedroom, she lays the five-foot-something pillow in the center of the bed. Surrounding it, leaning up against the headboard, is an atoll of throw pillows like those in the living room. Susan undresses herself in front of the full-length mirror. She is beautiful. Perfect face. Perfect breasts. She's glowing.

Her hands drift down to her gravid belly.

Going to have to pick up some cocoa butter for those stretchmarks she thinks.

Susan slides into bed, wrapping her arms around the body pillow. It's warm…so warm.

Mammals are always so –very- warm.

She reaches out and plucks a pillow from the headboard and cradles it. She begins to hum gently. It vibrates against her breast and begins to chirp. The other pillows shiver and take up the chorus.

"You're going to have some cousins soon, little one," she coos to it. "We're all going to be one big happy family, just like I had when I was little,"

She nuzzles the body pillow as the skin over her backbone splits with a wet, tearing sound. Susan's ovipositor pulls free from its confinement, trailing streamers of mucus and stretching, quivering, flexing over the bedspread.

"Emma, we're going to be *mommies*," she whispers.

The three foot long, curving, black stinger rears back and plunges deep inside.

"Baby, things have been rough lately, but I just *know* they're gonna get better."

Susan gasps as her abdomen pulses, the glow within tinged red by her distended flesh. She heaves and it contracts, sending thousands of eggs sluicing through the stinger. The body pillow starts to swell ever so slightly.

One big happy family.

The End.

CASE #47628

SOFT CELL

BY SEAN SPAGNOLI

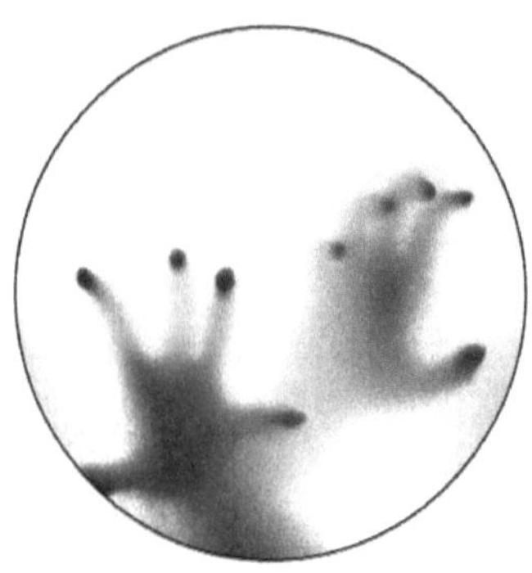

Sean Spagnoli is a gay scientist living in the wilds of Oregon. This is his first published work of fiction.

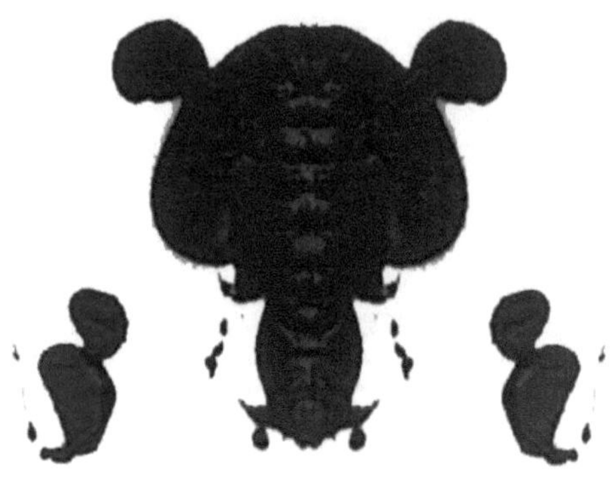

The Monster Maker by Adam Gaylord

A shuffle in the darkness, then a click and blinding light filled the room. Leather straps kept me pinned to the exam table, unable to turn toward the sound.

"Look who's finally awake," a voice creaked like a rusty door hinge.

"Who's there?" I tried to ask but could only a mumble around a foul-tasting gag.

"Yes, yes, I'm coming."

A silhouette swam briefly across my field of vision.

"Oh yes, definitely time to get started."

The strap across my forehead tightened painfully and then was gone. I looked around but could see very little outside the circle of white light illuminating the table from above. I craned my neck, trying to spot some clue as to where I was or who was holding me but no matter how I struggled, the straps didn't budge.

"Might as well settle down. We're going to be here a while," the voice chuckled. My captor seemed to find humor in that and the chuckle devolved into a maniacal laugh. "Unless you're afraid?" the voice crowed.

I clenched my jaw and try to shake my head, determined not to give this madman the pleasure of knowing my terror. The strap keeps my head from moving but he seemed to understand because the laugh cut off suddenly, silence hanging heavy in the air.

"That's a shame," the voice said, suddenly somber. "That's the problem with the world today – nobody's afraid."

A tray of shiny metal instruments, scalpels, saws, and plenty of things I couldn't name, wheeled into the light next to the table. Of who pushed the cart I could see only lab coat and gloved hands.

"You want to know why?" it asked. "Not enough monsters. Used to be, if you wanted your kid to stop screwing around and come home before dark, you just told him about the bogeyman." A loud scraping sound filled the room, metal on concrete.

Then a 55-gallon drum slid into the circle of light, a black and yellow radioactive symbol painted prominently on the side.

"The bogeyman. What a classic! A shape-shifter, that one. With a penchant for snatching little kids. They don't make 'em like that anymore. But ol' bogey passed back in '45. Cocaine overdose. Who knew?"

A sound I couldn't place hummed from the dark. Sweat stung my eyes and I clenched them shut, begging not to know what new horror approached. The humming grew and then cracked, grew and then cracked, all the while getting closer. When I couldn't take it any more I opened my eyes to find a series of coils perched above my head, electricity leaping between them in brilliant purple arcs.

"We won't need this until later." The arcs stopped and the humming silenced.

"Of course, the last wolf-man contracted rabies in '69," the voice continued from somewhere near my feet. "And most of the remaining vampires have either gone underground or gone Hollywood."

Squeaky wheels approached in the dark.

"The old guard's just about gone. Nobody left to scare kids into behaving. That's why the next generations gone to hell: no fear. No fear of the night. No fear of consequences, of retribution."

Two large cages squeaked into the light near my feet. In the first hung three large bats, their leathery wings wrapped around their hairy bodies. The second contained a baboon, instantly recognizable from its blue and red nose. It sat calmly, watching me with intelligent eyes, seemingly resolved to its fate.

"So, we'll give them something to fear," the voice cackled, apparently pleased once again. "Oh yes. We'll give them a monster the likes of which they've never seen before."

A tall figure stepped into the light. Behind the lab coat, gloves, and surgical mask I could see very little - only the eyes-cloudy, unblinking, and unseeing.

"You should be honored. You'll be doing your generation a great service."

The lights flickered and then were gone, my host apparently not needing them.

"Ok, let's get started. Oh, and I should warn you. This is really, *really* going to hurt."

And my transformation began.

The End.

CASE #:84808

THE MONSTER MAKER
BY ADAM GAYLORD

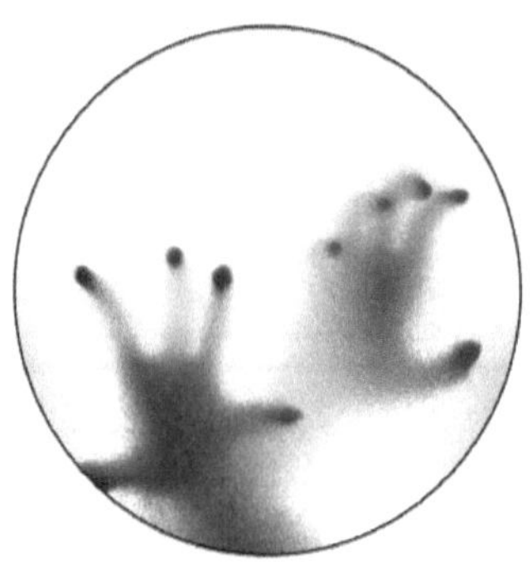

Adam Gaylord lives with his beautiful wife, daughter, and less beautiful dog in Colorado. When not at work as a biologist he's usually hiking, drinking craft beer, drawing comics, writing short stories, or some combination thereof. Check out his stuff at www.adamsapple2day.blogspot.com

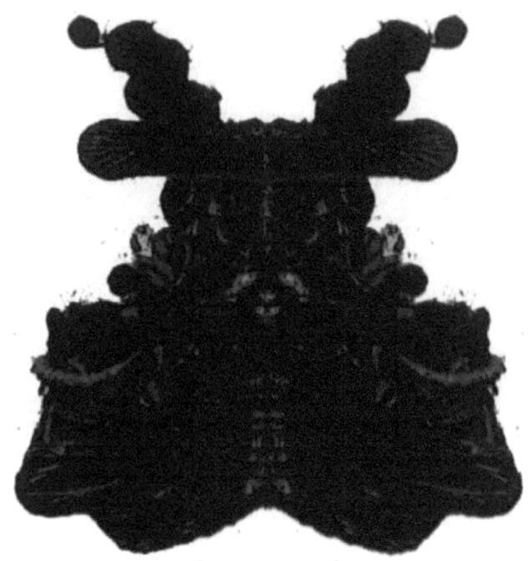

Devil Bird by Stephen Faulkner

The following are excerpts taken from the audio and written diaries of Dr. Flanders Jackson, Associate Professor of Physics, Gaylord College in Gaylord, Georgia.

It was a magnificent day for us when the window to UV-Zed was finally opened. We had been working out the theories and equations for nearly a year, then another year and a half designing a machine that would efficiently utilize our equations and guide the necessary energy so that a doorway or window to the universe parallel to our own could be opened without either killing us or destroying our own universe and everything in it in the process. Initially, we were afraid that the use of the amount of electrical energy that our calculations indicated as the minimum necessary for our plan to work could possibly cause an explosion that would, in the very least, level the entire Science Building and much of the surrounding campus of Gaylord College. The fact that I am writing this is evidence enough that such a calamity did not occur once the button was mashed and the stunning success of the project achieved.

Of course, there was little more that we could do once the window (or door) was opened in the center of the break room in our office suite. It hung in the air like a large elliptical balloon whose dimensions allowed it to touch both the floor and the ceiling and spread flatly (you could walk around it) to within three feet of the opposing walls. It chanted a gentle hum and gave off waves of static electricity that stood the hair on everyone's arms, chests and heads on end. Even Jenny, our department secretary, whose hair is quite long, looked utterly ridiculous with her ordinarily straight locks puffed out as if her head had grown three times larger while the size of her face remained normal. Everyone in the office had a good laugh at that, Jenny included once she was given a mirror.

The hiccoughing laughs and chortles stopped, though, when Addison's computer began ringing like a fire alarm, something it had never done before nor which it had ever been programmed to do. He hurried over and scanned the monitor and then, with a startled gasp, he tapped the keys to print out what he had seen glowing on the screen that had so astonished him.

"Take a look at this," he said when the printer had rolled out the single page communication just received. As each of us scanned what looked to be an official memo sent a short time ago sent from an office down the hall, each one of us, in turn, gasped at what we had just read.

****

FROM: The Office of Doctor Ekáshev Mulk

Director of the Inter-Universal Search Project Kraákol University of Chelv, Sek-Nemsh Province

TO: Esteemed Colleagues of the Xan-Flek Parallel Universe

We bid you greetings! Since our respective universes are parallel to one another and that we have opened a communications conduit between our two cosmi I am going by the assumption that we are much similar and so utilize a much similar language and writing. With this assumption comes the hope that my missive will be understood in this language that we call An-Galesha, which is translated from the Rectish tongue as (paraphrased), "of the house of Galesh." If your linguists speak so to us, I can put them in touch with those here who can go into more intellectual depth on the topic of Galesh and other languages of our world, Aerdeth, as the need and interest in such things is expressed.

Another assumption has here been made and this is that, since more than half the energy that has been estimated to achieve this end has been spent by us to open this conduit between our two cosmi, that both your team and ours are equally complicit in achieving this amazing and unprecedented feat of science. Congratulations to us all! Our physicists and technicians will, as we say, have to compare notes on the theories and mechanical means by which our corresponding processes were conducted and the opening of the cosmic portal realized.

Let this, then, be the end of our first communication, short though it may be. We welcome a response in whatever way in which you would like to couch it. Shall it be scientific in nature, or social, or evocative of your Aerdeth's languages, literatures and arts or, simply, a mere hello such as ours has been – we welcome whatever you would like to say to us.

All we ask is that a conversation between and among equals now be commenced.

Your Colleague Across the Void,
Doctor Ekáshev Mulk

***

Having read Doctor Mulk's letter twice I agonized only momentarily on what to say to this being from another universe. Two thoughts came to me almost simultaneously before I began to write my reply.

Dear Dr. Mulk,

Aren't you as amazed as I am about our being able to communicate with a person from not a different world but an entirely different universe from our own? There is still so much to study and learn about this phenomena we have created. I would greatly enjoy being able to sit with you face to face and ask and answer the innumerable amount of questions that I am sure both of us have swimming about in our brains. Right now the topmost question I have in mind is a technical one: Since the portal has been opened to electronic communications such as the one I am now writing, can it then be widened and enhanced to allow the passage of matter, as well? Of course I am specifically thinking of the passage of human beings to and from our respective cosmi. Tell me, has your team of technicians and researchers come up with any viable solution to this problem?

I would appreciate hearing back from you with your thoughts on this matter when your busy schedule permits.

Ever yours,

Dr. Flanders Jackson

Associate Professor of Physics;

Director, Applied Inter-Universal Study Project, Gaylord University

I considered that my communique may have sounded a bit stiff and formal but felt that it said and asked what I wanted it to. So, I hit the "send" key and hoped for the best that Ekáshev Mulk would choose to send in return. We did not have to wait long to hear what he had to say.

***

Colleague Flanders Jackson,

In my culture the term "Dear" is only utilized between members of the opposite sex who are presently intimately involved. I ask you not to use this word in reference to myself or any other Aerdethian individual for the great possibility of rendering an offence that you did not intend. Please make a note of it.

As for the possibility of opening the window between our individual comsi, I am sure that it can be done. Having said this, I would pray, for the sake of you and your people, your team and your colleagues and their families, that this venture not be attempted. We here in the Universi d'un, as we call our world and its position in the spiral of the galaxy Cream Road, have what might be labeled as a monster that bedevils our towns and cities at its evil whim. It is the great black feathered devil bird named Barukhá. This bird, some forty cubits in height with a wingspan perhaps thrice that, has been known to capture and gorf down the entire body of a living man so that for nearly an hour the tortuous cries of fatal suffering of that person would echo through the stomach and feather covered hide of the bird until the man finally expired. Barukhá has also been known to raise into the sky a heifer weighing some thirty drdls unshod and later gorge on its thick skin, meat, entrails and offal organs first as the animal lives and cries, yells and shits in its agony and later on the cooling, bloody corpse of the beast that has been thus killed. Often it would do such a dastardly thing within earshot of an entire town, giving nightmares to adults as well as children for many months to come.

This, then, is why we ask that you do not broach the subject of opening the door between our two realities: for the fear I hope I have instilled in you for possibility of the evil of Barukhá passing through the opened portal to your world. I hope that we will be able to share our respective wisdom, knowledge, culture and comradery via these communications that are much like the postal letters passed between friends and family members in my world. I do not wish share the vile, pernicious and violent evil that is Barukhá. Our friendship is too new for it to be so suddenly be consumed by the talons and razor beak of the devil Bird of Aerdeth.

Take good heed as I bid you all good health and happiness, gentle people of Xan-Flek.

Your Colleague,

Doctor Ekáshev Mulk

***

Having read Dr. Mulk's note on his people's unbelievably superstitious belief in a "devil bird," I sent the following note, feeling that honesty, as is said, is the best policy. Another "as they say" is *Let the chips fall where they may.*

Doctor Mulk,

As you can see from the above that I have taken to heart your advice on how to couch a salutation to an individual residing in your universe, or cosmi, as you put it.

Regarding the warning that runs through the rest of your communication I have to be honest in telling you that, even prior to reading your letter, my team has already worked out the mathematical basés for opening the portal so as to allow matter transference between our universes as well as the waves and particles of our typed messages to one another. The legends and myths of such beasts as your Barukhá are seen in my world for what they are — myths and legends; stories to teach our children in a symbolic manner of the imminent pitfalls of a dangerous world. All rational adults here are cognizant of the need for dragons and evil serpents in the garden and trolls and ogres without believing that such beings truly exist.

My team will work on devising the electronic means of opening the door between our worlds, or cosmi, and will most likely have it operational within a day or two. I hope that you and your team will do the same so as to minimize the drain on the power sources at your end that will be necessary to have this phase of what has become our joint project come to fruition.

I am certain I will hear from you soon.

Ever yours,

Dr. Flanders Jackson

Associate Professor of Physics;

Director, Applied Inter-Universal Study Project, Gaylord University

***

And his surprisingly unemotional reply:

Are you under the assumption that I and my team as well as the entire population of Aerdeth still live in the Back Ages where superstition is endemic throughout the land? Believe me when I tell you, Sir, that Barukhá is no mere myth or legend or flight of the collective imagination of my people. Barukhá is the last of his kind and though, yes, there have been tales and legends written about him, the bird itself is alarmingly real and of great danger to humanity. My last missive was but a warning to you that, should Barukhá come through my lab (whose doors are now always open to allow the pleasant passage of a summer zephyr to pass through and thus lessen the power burden that would be the result of overuse of our climate control system), then the terror of having Barukhá as your own devil bird would become a horrific reality for your world. A warning, sir; a warning from one colleague and friend to another.

But my team members have just now made me aware that you have already started the sequence to open the portal between us. Should we choose not to cooperate, all your efforts will come to naught without the aid of our additional power source coming to the fore to get this job done. You have made your decision in this and we respect that. We shall help as best we can. Your sequencing has been received and encoded into our system.

And to reiterate: this was only a warning, Sir. No ultimatum in any way was in any way intended.

Your Friend and Colleague,
Doctor Ekáshev Mulk

***

Rick Addison, Carl Ruhar, Corey Chenowith and I had a discussion that ranged from moments of humor and acceptance to disbelief and near anger at the "culture" of the people of Aerdeth that would allow such a superstition to proliferate and become an accepted reality.

"Maybe it's not a mythic reality for them like the gods were for the Greeks and Romans," said Addison, sounding like he had been trying to come up with a sensible reason. "Maybe it's more like the Golem for the Jews or lycanthropy for the Eastern Europeans. They believe it even though they're aware that it doesn't have any true realness to it."

"I'm not sure of your analogies," said Chenowith. "But I see what you mean."

"Who the hell cares about the whats and wherefores of the Aerdethian belief system?" Ruhar piped up with a sentiment we all seemed to share. "It's there, we deal with it and we go forward."

"Deal with it?" I asked.

"Yeah," he said. "Deal with it. I mean recognize that that's what they believe – then go ahead with the project as planned."

"You mean totally discount their warnings altogether?" said Addison.

Ruhar touched his nose with the forefinger of his right hand and pointed at Addison with a wink.

"It's really a load of superstitious bullshit when you come down to it, like Carl said," Chenowith commented.

"So we just hit the switch and set the plan in motion as we had originally planned?" I said. "Even though we'll be pulling enough juice to fry the grid in this area when we do it?"

Ruhar shrugged. "That was the risk we knew we'd be taking before we figured that we had the Aerdethian's side of things to pick up half the slack."

"I say we do it," said Addison. "Let Mulk and his people stew in their own superstitious pot of stew." Everyone groaned and made faces at his weird metaphor. "All right, all right," he chanted embarrassedly. "But you know what I mean."

"Okay then," I said. "Is that what everyone fells about this?" I got nods all around as my answer. "So let's do this, then. Rick, set the sequence to divert full power to the main series. Carl, be sure to monitor flow. Corey, keep your hand on the trigger so you can hit it as soon as Corey gives you the go sign. We all ready?"

"Aye, Cap'n," Ruhar, the comedian of the crew and sounding like Scotty from the old Star Trek TV series, said.

"Then let's do this!"

"Sequencing power at quarter level," Addison called, opening the sequencing pattern. "And up a tenth … and two … and to the half mark…."

And so it began.

***

Almost immediately upon the commencement of our sequencing drill a communiqué from Mulk rang through on Addison's computer. "Damn!" said Chenowith. "That guy must have taken a speed typing course when he was in high school. What's it been? Thirty seconds or something since we started?"

"Now, boys," I said, mock angry as I brought Mulk's note up on the screen. "Play nice, no pissy insults to our friends in other universes."

Mulk's note was much as I expected to be:

Esteemed, Ignorant Colleague, it began, totally negating my adjuration on not using pissy insults.

It has come to our attention here that you have already begun the countdown to opening the portal on your own in utter disregard to my warning of the danger that you face. We hear the wings of Barukhá's swift approach even as I write this.

Since your action has the consequential result that our power grid will also be affected we are forced to either shut off communication with you altogether so as to minimize any danger to us and our power supply, or else follow your foolish lead and allow the portal to be opened. Being a scientist who wants his project to be seen through to its successful conclusion, I choose the latter scenario. Our progression now is in effect, as well.

Barukhá is loudly beating at the outside door to our lab, seeking ingress. When the progression here reaches critical and the portal must be cleared for opening, it shall be done. At the same time the door of this laboratory will be opened to allow Barukhá his will to seek new worlds, new prey. Understand that I do this not out of malice to you and your kind, but for the preservation of my own people. The result shall be that Barukhá will be yours with which to contend.

I have been given word that the progression has reached its limit, as has that on your side. I pray for you to all our godhead figures in all our religions for you, your family and your race, Colleague Flanders Jackson. Live long, be well, and accept my sincerest apology with the understanding of why this thing has been done.

Sincerely,

Doctor Ekáshev Mulk

And we all watched in fascination as the inter-universal portal irised open to its full width with a Gregorian hum.

***

The first thing we heard was the beating of wings. There was no way of knowing if the volume of the sound was due to the echoing effect of a closed in space or if the sound was as actually as loud as it seemed. At first the sound issued forth as from a great distance but quickly rose in volume to a pitch that can only be described as thunderous. *Thrup-thrup–pock!* as his foot caught purchase, then, *Thrup-thrup-thrup-pock!* once again, and again *Thrup-thrup-thrup-thrup-pock! Pock!* The slow, even, maddeningly elongating cadence as it made its way closer and closer to coming into our world, our universe.

Each of us muttered his own individual epithets as Barukhá came through the passageway to the portal from its universe to ours. "Whoa!" was Corey's favorite word in times of stress and he used it easily now. "Holy shit!" said Rick with a hand over his mouth and Carl said nothing but just poked his tongue daintily out of his mouth and spit a saliva laced raspberry fricative into the mix.

"Oh boyoboyoboy," is all I was able to whisper as we waited for this devil bird of Aerdeth to make his vaunted entrance into our realm.

"I COME!" came the raspy voice shouting from the humming portal.

"Holy shit, oh shit, oh shit…" Rick litanized fearfully while the rest of us, if not cowering in our seats, were lost in silent reverie or, in my case, in prayer.

"HUNGRY-EE-EE-EE…!" echoed the harsh, parrot like voice as if electronically enhanced. "Hungry for flesh!!"

"Gun!" chirped Rick in a panic of insight to a solution. "Is there a gun in this lab? Does anyone have a gun?"

"A pocketknife is all I have," said Carl lugubrious, his earlier mouth farting panic now lost. "No gun."

"Firearms aren't allowed anywhere on campus," I reminded him.

"Whuh-what are we gonna do, then?" Corey asked in a shaky voice. "We gotta do something to protect ourselves."

"Close the portal!" Rick suggested in a madly frightened voice, too high and too loud.

"FEED ME!" yelled the bird, too close for comfort now. "I Come-M-M-M-m-m-m…."

"That's it," said Carl. "Close the damned door. Cut its head off."
"Don't be idiots," I said, trying to be the voice of reason, the one to remind them of protocol. "Once the progression has finished and

the door is open, we have to wait at least three hours to reverse the process. You all know that!"

"Oh shit, oh shit, oh shit...!" chanted Rick while Corey whispered

"whoa!" about five times in quick succession and Carl spit farted a lengthy razz that went on and on until....

We saw him, the great devil bird Barukhá, poking his immense beak out of the portal, then studied us with the liquid black pupil of his beady eye.

Then he came all the way through, flew into our laboratory and made a circuit around the perimeter defined by the four walls. And landed with a final Pock! which must have been the sound made by the locking of its leg joints as it landed…. Right on my shoulder.

The bird, through ugly of mien, was about the size of the average earthly crow.

"Oh damn!" it exclaimed as it shit on my shoulder. And then it took off through the only window of the lab and flew toward the tree line that formed the border of the college campus.

***

The party that ensued with the project teams of both Universe UV-Zed and Xan-Flek attending lasted three hours and consumed an entire bottle of moscato wine. Dr. Mulk and his team of two young graduate assistants averaged a mere three inches in height, like the soldiers or cowboys in a little boy's war or western playset, so it was quite apparent why the population of their world was so terrified of the appearance of Barukhá . All three got totally, blindingly drunk on but a thimbleful of wine. We made beds for them out of a pile of cotton that we use for cleaning the delicate electronics of our computers and blankets out of the soft cloth used to keep the monitors and flat surfaces clean. After a nap of about three hours our guests made their way back through the portal to their own universe.

After a few hours for our new friends' to nurse their hangovers communications began once more. The first one was a plea to close the portal to all solid matter transference. The suggestion was voted on and unanimously approved. Since we were already beyond the three-hour waiting period, it was done immediately. Communication between our two universes (or cosmi, as Ekáshev has termed them) will continue as before. The only time the portal will be reopened to solid matter will be if and when there comes a new Barukhá in Universe UV-Zed. We are only too happy to lend aid to our friends in alleviating the giant pest problem in their Lilliputian frame of reference.

After all, one bird, more or less, in this universe will make no real difference. Will it?

The End.

CASE #28752
DEVIL BIRD
BY STEPHEN FAULKNER

Stephen Faulkner is a guy who loves to write fiction that takes the world apart and puts it back together in interesting and imaginative ways.

He also loves to share his talent with all who appreciate his singular style. He lives in Decatur, Georgia with his wife and five cats.

Steve has published stories in Aphelion Webzine, Unhinged Magazine, Hellfire Crossroads, Temptation Magazine, Hobo Pancakes,

The Erotic Review, Serendipity Magazine, Liquid Imagination and Dreams Eternal.

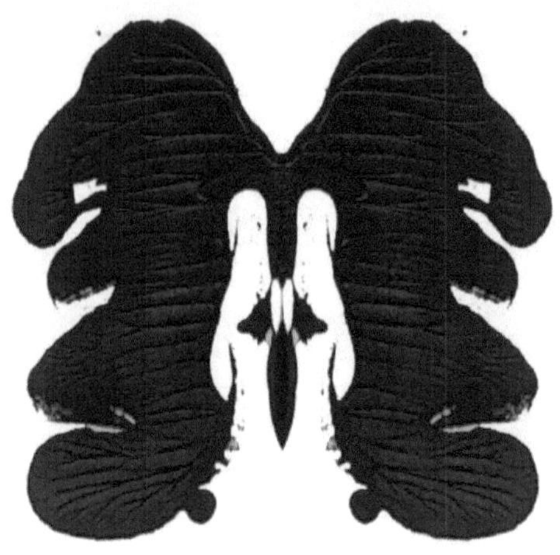

Her Presence Covered In Mist by Elmedina Hota

Her pallor gleams under the midnight skies,

her beauty indescribable,

wrapped by the nocturnal mist, on the cold ground she lies,

so pure and dreamy, to human's flesh unreachable...

Devils in orchestra played symphonies of Hell to her,

admiring her figure, for her Death they linger, the countess shall

be killed, then again she'll rise, the melody grows heavier as she

slowly dies

Her presence is covered in mist,

through which she mourns to the darkened sky, she's lost her

soul the first time she was kissed by an angel whose dark wings

are too heavy to fly.

To Hell she'll go along with her loyal pipers, nothing to infix

the fear as a lovely, steadfast vipers, an evil creature shall

follow her as her slave, to crawl for her and spread the poison

in her cave, to slay the beautiful, slice the roots of hope, 666

shall be her heal, no longer for the light she'll grope

'I shall take away the tranquility of the guiltless creatures, metamorphose it into the terror and scorn, for my

vengeance shall have the most bitter features, still honest

is my heart that once used to burn.

Nightmares shall wear my name, every

mortal shall feel that flame,

the mutilation of mind once the evil rise,

mark my words.'

Her presence is covered in mist,

through which she mourns to the darkened sky, she's lost

her soul the first time she was kissed

by an angel whose dark wings were too heavy to fly.

CASE #: 85757

HER PRESENCE COVERED IN MIST
BY ELMEDINA HOTA

I am an artist based in Sarajevo, Bosnia and Herzegovina.

I started taking interest in photography around the age of fourteen. That makes it ten years of learning and developing photography skills I have today.

With photography, I naturally started to experiment with make-up and fashion. In fact, I finished a high school of fashion design, and even though I didn't go for a licence in make-up artistry, I do it professionally in beauty and hair salon "Mig" in Sarajevo, BiH.

I also do it around Halloween when people are interested in horror face paints, which I enjoy doing.

I started writing when I was eighteen years old. I was deeply influenced by the music of Cradle of Filth, Theatres des Vampires, Lord Vampyr, Saturnus... Being inspired by these artists, I discovered I have a few things to write down myself.

Scenarios and other-worldly imagery ran through my mind, and as I was writing, I felt free.

No limits, no restrictions. I could've made anything come to life. And so I did.

„Her Presence Covered In Mist" is the third poem I ever wrote. It gives me great joy to see people appreciate something that I was able to produce, something that I would once consider to be not much more than a fragment of my mind.

A Fall Poem by James Michael Shoberg

Dear Noah loved the autumn—oh, that season, crisp and cool,

A harbinger to others of another year in school.

But Noah never understood their misery and grief.

He'd gladly trade the summer for a single tinted leaf.

Despite his comrades' sense of loss, and urge to gripe and

grouse, They'd humor him, remembering what grew behind

his house.

For there lived an impressive oak, and regally it stood.

Upon its boughs, a kid could see beyond the neighborhood.

And it was from this vantage point, ablaze with harvest hue,

That they would watch the dimming sun recede as darkness
grew.

Yet Noah, feeling cheated, knew he couldn't share these sights.

He wished that he could join them, but he had a fear of heights.

"This isn't fair! The tree is mine—the time of year as well!"

Though just a fleeting skyward glance turned Noah's legs to gel.

His pals began to taunt and tease with catcalls from above:

"Hey, Noah! You should see the view! It's one you'd surely

love! Boy, look at all those pretty leaves—the scarlet, orange,

gold— And we can spot them, every one. Too bad you're not as

bold." Like monkeys they sat gibbering among the colored

spray. "How is it they're unruffled, while their perches bend and sway?! If they can do it," Noah thought, "then so can I! Be brave!"

But all at once, his face took on a mien profoundly grave.

He filled his lungs with evening air (which smacked a bit of smoke),

And stood there in the shadow of that overwhelming oak.

Determined, Noah scaled the trunk without another thought,

Each hand sought out a sturdy branch, each foot, a bulging knot.

They'd see was courageous if he met them at the top.

"But twilight's fading quickly, so I mustn't slow or st—" "STOP!

That limb has splintered, Noah, and it's in a fragile state! We

broke it climbing up ourselves! It cannot bear your weight!"

Those tardy words of warning were drowned out by Noah's

gasp, As in that very instant, it had snapped off in his grasp.

It compromised his balance when the shoot tore from the bark,

And Noah flailed but failed to find a second, stronger mark.

He pitched and plunged at rapid pace, bathed in a tawny glow.

All he could do was pray the leaves would cushion him below.

"I raked them into ample piles. Lord, make them nice and dense."

But piles and prayers did little good. He cleared the neighbor's fence.

And while the space beneath the tree was soft and yielding
yard,

The area he landed on was concrete, flat and hard.

But Noah's end was festive—yes, his pumpkin of a head
Burst open in a surge of yellow mixed with bloody red.

A vivid stew of brains and gore began to blend and clot.

The colors would have pleased him, for he'd fancied them a lot.

His friends observed from far above the gooey, gluey scene.

One said, "I guess he's going as a ghost for Halloween."

CASE #41654

A FALL POEM
BY JAMES MICHAEL SHOBERG

James Michael Shoberg is a director, designer, and award-winning actor and playwright. His writing credits include numerous fringe plays and collections of both monologues and poems. James is also the Co-Executive Producer, Artistic Director, and Resident Playwright of The Rage of the Stage Players, a fringe theatre company in Pittsburgh, Pennsylvania. In 2011, he received the permission of The Butcher Brothers and Lionsgate Films to write, produce, and direct a world-premiere stage adaptation of their award-winning independent horror film, The Hamiltons, for The Rage of the Stage Players. James' unique brand of twisted theatre has already attracted attention both nationally and internationally. His most recent endeavor is a currently untitled book of horror poetry for young adults, excerpts of which have appeared in Beyond the Nightlight, Cellar Door III: Animals Anthology, Pavor Nocturnus Dark Fiction Anthology, Phobos Magazine, Sanitarium Magazine, and Under the Bed Magazine, to name a few.

On the.
Record

Three million books in twenty countries? Amazing! Congrats. Have you ever tried to read any of your books after they have been translated into a different language?

I have. They're much better when I can't understand a word I've written.

What do you think attracts audiences to the horror, mystery and sci-fi genres? Do you think these audiences differ much from, say, romance or non-fiction?

A book is a way to vicariously experience emotion. It's like a test run of the limbic system. Some people like to be frightened,  or puzzled, or placed in worlds unlike their own. Some like the thrill of vicariously falling in love, or turned on. Some consider information to be entertainment.

It's all personal preference, and it's all good.

What is your favorite non-horror genre to read? Do you get to do much reading for pleasure?

Other than non-fic, most of my reading is my peers, sending me stuff to review. It's sort of like a magician watching other magicians. We all know the secrets and tricks, and it's more about finding the weaknesses in order to be helpful than it is appreciating the strengths. So I haven't really read fiction for pleasure in years.

But I'm a sucker for movies. It doesn't matter if I feel I can guess what will happen next, I still fall victim to the narrative. Which is great.

When your work is awarded, as yours has been many times, does it inspire you to continue to produce better work? Or does it reinforce that what you're doing is working, and you build upon that?

Awards, or reviews, or sales, are indicators that the work is working. The fun is in forcing yourself to stretch beyond your comfort zone and try something different. I like to think that each of my novels is unique, and will hopefully surprise the reader as much as it challenged me to produce.

What is the craziest thing a fan has ever written to you about or sent you?

I had a fan who had her tombstone inscribed with a line from one of my novels. I never expected to be someone's epitaph. I also had a fan tell me I should be euthanized, because they didn't like a joke in one of my stories.

Tell us a little about the Kindle Worlds project. How did that begin?

The idea behind Kindle Worlds is allowing writers to play in each other's' sandboxes. For example, I'd love to be able to write a James Bond novel, or a Travis McGee, just for the fun of it. But those intellectual properties are owned by rightsholders who won't allow it. So a few years ago I decided to allow writers to use my characters, with limited restrictions. It was similar to what Kindle Worlds was doing, but with a vital difference; I allowed writers to keep their rights.

Amazon was smart enough to allow that idealogy to transfer over when I joined their KW program, and now many other KW authors are doing the same thing.

What has been your favorite book to write? Do you have a least favorite?

I love writing the Timecaster books, which is funny because they're easily the least successful thing I've ever done. But they allow my imagination to fully run rampant, and to stick in a lot of theoretical science and futurist stuff, which I enjoy a lot.

As for least favorite, I wrote a book called Disturb with the intent to write in a style that wasn't my own. My books, even the erotica and the horror, always have humor in them. Disturb did not. As such, I didn't enjoy the process as much. Life is funny. We should laugh whenever we can.

We love your "Newbie's Guide to Publishing Blog"! What advice would you give rising young authors above all else? Do you believe the world of self-publishing and e-books has helped more young authors get their start?

Writers need to focus on writing. Get those words on the page. Write until you get to the end, and then start the next project. Worrying too much about social media, or self-promotion, takes away from your writing time.

When I got started, I had to impress gatekeepers; agents and editors. I got over five hundred rejections and wrote ten novels before selling anything. This was a depressing time, but it also was trial by fire. I had to improve in order to succeed.

Today, writers don't need to jump through hoops to reach an audience. All we need to do is press a button to publish. That's great, and it's also dangerous. If I'd had that power back in 1992, I would have self-pubbed my first book. But that would have been a mistake; it was rejected for a reason.

Self-pubbing, and Amazon in particular, has helped a lot of writers earn some money, and reach readers, for the very first time. But if your work isn't ready, you're sabotaging your own career before it even starts. Make sure you know your craft before you release your baby into the world.

Why have you chosen to write using pseudonyms at times?

Publishers. They wanted different names for different genres, because they were too short-sighted to believe my mystery fans would follow me if I wrote horror, or sci-fi.

I chose a pen name for my erotica because I was working with a co-author, and because we wanted to see if we could sell on the strength of the book rather than the strength of our brand. It was a fun experiment, and we did well.

In hindsight, I should have insisted on putting "Joe Konrath" on all of my books. I have fans who want to read everything but are confused which books are mine. It would have been simpler to just be me.

What is your favorite non-literary activity?

Craft beer. I have a beer cellar large enough to get me through a nuclear winter.

What does 2016 have in store (release wise) for yourself?

Two new Jack Daniels thriller novels, Rum Runner and Last Call, and a horror novel called WebCam. They should all be out by spring—assuming I can stay away from my cellar long enough to finish them…

A little more about Joe:

Joe Konrath has sold more than two million books in twenty countries. He's written over thirty novels and over a hundred short stories in the mystery, thriller, horror, and sci-fi genres. Known for combining incredible action, hair-raising scares, and big laughs, Konrath has received over 10,000 Amazon reviews for his work, averaging 4.2 stars out of 5. He's been a #1 Amazon bestseller on three different occasions, and has been in the Top 100 bestseller lists over twenty times.

http://jakonrath.com/

What was the catalyst that gave you the bug to write? Have you always had the urge to be creative?

My poor parents. I was always writing. My mother worked late at the local newspaper, and she'd take me to the office with

her. I had to entertain myself, so I'd roam the halls and write on the typewriters. I was always making up stories. I very much lived inside of my head instead of the Real World. The Real World was a bit too harsh for me. After graduating college, I decide to become an adult and get a real job. It took me several years to get back to writing, and I'll never walk away again.

You're a self-proclaimed writer of a multitude of genres: poetry, short stories, essays, etc. Do you have a favorite?

Flash fiction has a special place in my heart. I adore novels because you can add all of the detail you want, but the opposite is true in flash. It's a great exercise in making every word count. Every detail is there for a reason and there is no room for anything extraneous. It's a very lean form, and I love the challenge of it.

We have to know the story behind your website's name, *A Broken Laptop*. Where did that come from?

 Oh my goodness! Well, my son ate most of the keys off of my first laptop. I wrote my first novel without being able to see any of the letters, and hitting the nubby part of the button with my fingers because the keys were gone. My friend says he wants to get me a military grade laptop because they're virtually indestructible. I've gone through at least four of mine. I type with passion and ferocity.

What do you think the fascination with murder as a genre of mystery is so big? Why has it always fascinated audiences?

 Murder is unthinkable to most of us. It's the worst of the worst. You can do anything else to a human, no matter how horrific, and someone will say, "At least they're alive." Murder is such a dark path that it's naturally thrilling to people. The genre is a way to read about it and flirt with the danger without committing to it in any real way. I think it also helps us stare into the face of horror and work through some of our own feelings without being harmed. It's cathartic.

Do you have a secret formula in your writing for blending your "dark and beautiful" stories? Why do those two seemingly work so well together?

You need to find the beauty in the darkness or you'll go mad. You'll simply break. Flowers grow from corpses. People emerge from horror stronger than they were before. Beauty and darkness are intertwined.

There is no specific formula for me. My job as an author is to keep my eyes open, and the gorgeous dichotomy of horror and beauty show themselves to me. It's how I see the world, and how I've always seen it. Things and people you love will hurt you. Whatever you care for breaks. How do you live through that? You find the loveliness in the shattered pieces, and in that same regard, realize that those breathtaking pieces will cut you.

What is the strangest job you've ever had to support your writing career?

There were probably two of those. I worked at a plasma center in downtown Seattle, and I met the strangest characters. I also worked in a sex offender home for boys ages 13-21. I was 21 at the time, so some of the kids there were my age. That was a thing of nightmares. In fact, I still have terrible dreams about that place.

With three kids, it must be difficult to get the time in to write! What do your kids think of your work, and how do they influence you?

96

Time is definitely precious! I don't have time for long, lingering phone calls or lazy lunches.

The kids are pretty cool with it. My eight-year-old has read a few of my books and brings them to school. The Littlest knows I like horror shows. They get excited when we make voodoo doll cookies or when I get a medieval dagger in the mail. Kids roll with it better than adults do. And they're so creative! I've based

characters on the kids themselves, or on things the kidlets have told me. The Tip-Toe Shadow, a villain in *Nameless: The Darkness Comes* was based on a shadow that my little girl said talked to her at night. "He walks on his tip toes and says mean things." Quite horrifying and inspiring. People have written and said how badly Tip-Toe scared them. He terrified me, too, when I first heard of him.

How important is cover art to you and your work? What does that process look like for you?

Cover art is quite important to me. The process kind of goes like this: "Hey, George, what do you have?" George Cotronis has done quite a few of my covers. He has this deconstructed nuts-and-bolts style that still manages to be dreamlike. I approached Galen Dara for *Pretty Little Dead Girls'* cover because her work is so feminine with a definite creep factor. I try to find an artist that fits the work, and then let them do their stuff. I tried to micromanage once with *Beautiful Sorrows,* and I realized that instead of giving Yannick Bouchard ideas, I was merely beating the creativity out of him. So I'll tell the artist what the book is about, describe key scenes so they have an idea of vibe, and let them do what they do.

I've been exceptionally fortunate to have stunning book covers thanks to these amazing artists. I couldn't be happier.

Covers are so important that when I left one publisher and went with a new one, I paid for my covers to come with me.

Do you think it's harder or easier for female writers in the horror/mystery genre to break out into their career or to be taken seriously? Do you feel there are any gender biases in this area of creative writing?

Ooh, that's a loaded question. And especially for Women in Horror month.

I think it's harder to break out as a female. Although there are fantastic female writers like Mary Shelley, Joyce Carol Oates, and Shirley Jackson, women are still viewed as newcomers to the horror genre. It's a "good ole' boys" playground and that's a difficult mindset to get away from.

At the same time, there's a revolution going on that seeks to change this. Female-only anthologies, Women in Horror month, the HWA scholarship for a female writer...all of these things are being done to let people know that the ladies are here and they're valued. That's a great thing. But of course there are biases, just like there are biases against male romance writers. It isn't that a man can't write a wonderful, 

thoughtful, creative romance, because of course they can. But there is a stigma against it, just as there is still a stigma against female horror writers.

What was your favorite subject in school? Has it inspired you to incorporate that subject matter into any of your work?

My favorite subject was, of course, creative writing. But I also loved chemistry. I remember sitting in class discussing exactly what formulas are used to make certain colors in fireworks, and that was so fascinating to me. I have a short story called "Wings" that mentions that. Everything that intrigues me ends up in my work somehow. It's sprinkled with little gems from real life.

What does 2016 have in store (release-wise) for you?

It's a crazy year for me! I have two books coming out in February. They are *Pretty Little Dead Girls*, which is a whimsical fairytale with a high body count, and *Apocalyptic Montessa and Nuclear Lulu: A Tale of Atomic Love*, which is sort of a Romeo and Juliet/Stephen King's *Firestarter* type of thing. Both are wonderful books that I'm proud of, and they're being re-released by Crystal Lake Publishing.

In July Crystal Lake is releasing book two in the BONE ANGEL trilogy. In September we're releasing the third and final book in the series. I'm writing like crazy. It's about all I do, but I like staying busy.
Thank you so much for the interview! It was a pleasure.

A little More about Mercedes:
Hi. I'm Mercedes. I have two broken laptops, three kids, a husband and no time to write, although I try my very best. I like to write stories. I like to write poems. I like to write essays and sometimes they're funny, sometimes they aren't. I'm the author of the short story collection Beautiful Sorrows, the "serial killers in love" novella Apocalyptic Montessa and Nuclear Lulu: A Tale of Atomic Love, my debut novel Nameless: The Darkness Comes, and Pretty Little Dead Girls: A

Novel of Murder and Whimsy. I specialize in the dark and beautiful.

https://abrokenlaptop.com

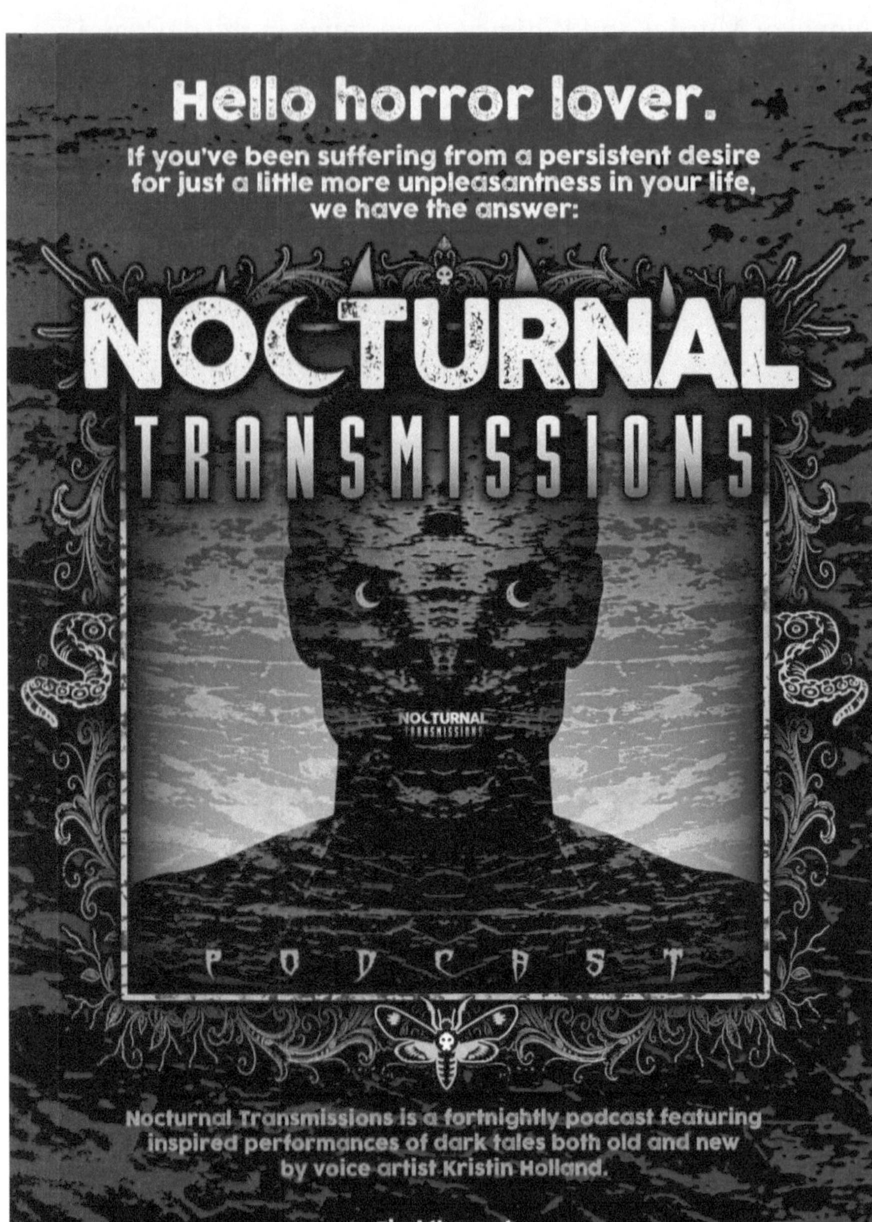

If you have any feedback or would like to leave a review please head over to Amazon and share your thoughts about Sanitarium.

Thank you for your time and we salute your love for all things horror.

https://www.facebook.com/SanitariumPublishing

https://www.thesanitarium.co.uk/

https://twitter.com/sanitariumlit

https://www.instagram.com/sanitariumpublishing/